GONE

A Novel By

Carrington W. Grant

Author's Note

This novel was inspired by Carrington's love for horror movies. Is 2nd favorite time of the year is Halloween because he loves to watch horror movies in theaters or at home with his family.

Fun Fact

Carrington Grant has been playing the drums since he was 3. He took private lessons until he was 14 and played in the school band.

DEDICATION

This book is dedicated to my parents, my mother, my sister, my grandparents and the rest of my supportive family.

ACKNOWLEDGEMENTS

I would like to thank my family and all my English language arts and reading teachers.

Prologue

It was always something. One day Grant was at school and out of nowhere all he heard was "There has been an intruder reported in the building please report to your safeguard locations. Apparently some guy dressed up as a monster tried to get into the school.

Grant woke up out of nowhere. The day that he had been dreading for the past 2 months was before him. Moving Day. He got out of bed and tripped on the dozens of boxes that were surrounding his room. His day was already off to a rough start. He was leaving his whole life behind him to move to a weird old town that he had no idea about. His whole family was excited about the move; especially his Mother Jane, and his brother J.J.

"Grant you should be downstairs by now; we are all waiting for you." his mother yelled. Grant sighed. He knew there was no avoiding what was already set in stone.

Grant and his family ate their final meal in their house although he ate nothing. His mind was too full of thoughts of his future and the effects of this big change. The family loaded up the moving truck and set off towards their new house. His father drove, his mother sat in the passenger seat, and Grant and his brother sat in the back.

"I was doing some research about the house" JJ said "it says here that the previous owners were run out of the house by a mysterious intruder. That's interesting! Who do you think it was?"

"It was obviously a burglar." Grant said. "What if the house is haunted and the mysterious intruder is some kinda ghost." JJ whispered. "That's that T.V crap that you get stuck on.

Everyone knows that ghosts aren't real your bonehead." Grant said. "Stop bickering you two. I do not want to hear that for the next 4 hours." Jane said. "I have heard great things about the house, it is a great neighborhood. Great school, park, and they have a public recreation center so you all can go play basketball whenever you all want to."

The Plan

The school bell rang. "Finally the end of another awful school day" thought Grant.

He was not particularly fond of a lot of things that went on in his life. He went to a weird school with weird kids. He lived with a weird family and most of all, he lived in a weird neighborhood. That was the one thing... his neighborhood. He always received a weird vibe from it. The only thing that he liked about it was that he lived so close to his two best friends -- George and Brian. They have been best friends since elementary school. And every year they look forward to the same time of year...Halloween. Every year they dress up and go trick-or-treating until their pillow cases are overflowing. They know people think it's a little strange that 14-year-old boys still dress up in costumes but they love every bit of it, and this year it was going to be different they had something grand planned.

"Alright so does everyone have the plan" said Grant at the lunch table.

"Yep" said George.

"Wait so we are meeting at Grant's House" Brian said unsurely.

"No your dodo we are meeting at George's house; we have been going over this for the past 2 months." Grant said.

"Ok ok, I got it" said Brian".

" Probably stuck gazing off into the distance thinking about Myaaa..." uttered George as if they were still in middle school.

"Shut-up, no I wasn't!" said Brian slamming is hands on the table.

The bell rang and Grant, Brian and George left the lunch table with one thing in mind -- Halloween.

Everything seemed to go slower than normal in school for Grant. It felt as if the school day would never come to an end. From class to class Grant went and finally it was the end of the day. Grant rushed home as fast as he could. Everything had to go smoothly for the plan to work and Grant knew it.

"Hey sweetie how was your day --I" said Grant's Mom Jane

"No time mom" said Grant as he rushed through the door. "Today is the biggest day of the year and everything must go as planned".

"I'm making roasted pumpkin seeds I know you can't resist your favorite Halloween snack, do you at least--" said Jane

"NO" said Grant as he sprinted to his room.

As Grant walked into his room everything seemed okay until the one thing that in needed for Halloween was missing.

"J.Jayyyyy !" Grant screamed from his room.

"What do you want" said J.J. "before you even say it I did not do it".

"Where the hell is my costume" said Grant.

"I didn't take it; you know I don't care about all that Halloween crap anyway." said J.J.

Grant walked back in his room to check again for his Halloween costume, "Oh I found it," said Grant.

Grant put on his costume. His bright red eyes could be seen from 1 mile away. His snarling mask would be sure to put a scare on everyone's face. Knowing his brother J. J's dislike of Halloween, he thought of the brilliant idea to scare him. He tiptoed to his brother's room.

"Rarrr !" Grant screamed. His brother jumped.

"Don't do that, why do you even have that on mom is not letting you go trick-or-treating" J.J said.

"Why not" said Gant.

"We have a Halloween party to go to and you're going" said J.J.

Grant erupted with tears and stormed into the kitchen.

"MOM!", cried Grant.

"Yes sweetie" said Grant's Mom.

"Do I have to go with you guys, George, Brian and I were going to go trick or treating" said Grant.

"Of course you have to go with us, it is a family event" said Grant's mom "Now go upstairs and get ready!"

"But--" Grant uttered. "I don't want to hear it" she replied.

Grant stormed upstairs with an alternate plan in mind. Grant went into his closet and pulled out a black duffle bag he filled it with Halloween costume, a pillowcase, and a rolled up piece of paper that said "The Plan" on it.

Minutes later Grant was halfway out the window using his tied up bed sheets as a rope. He repelled down the side of the side of the house ever so slyly making sure to not alarm his brother or worse his mother. "Alright 1 mile starting now" said grant determinately. He would rather walk than not go so that's what he decided to do.

Grant set off. As he walked he saw everyone's Halloween decorations. Everyone's yards were filled with skeletons, ghouls, and ghost. Grant loved it, he loved Halloween. Everything about it: The fun, The festivities, The candy. Sadly, the only people who celebrates it with him are his friends. His family wants nothing to do with it. They either always find something to do on Halloween other than Halloween things or stay home and do nothing. They don't even put out candy for the neighbors, it puts a sickening feeling in Grant's stomach. As grant got closer and closer to George's house his heartbeat started to rise. He could feel is plan coming to fruition.

Grant stepped on George's porch and rang the doorbell. Seconds later George and Brian opened the door with a wide grin on the two of their faces. "Operation October is a go" grant said returning the grin to two of them.

The three boys walked to George's bed room.

"How did you even get here" said Brian "I didn't see your Mom's car".

"I know this may sound crazy" Grant said "But I snuck out the house".

"Dude your crazy" said George.

"Didn't I just say that" Grant said. The three laughed. "I know it sounds crazy but it was for a good reason".

"Which was...?" uttered George.

"Basically my mom wanted me to go to some lame family event with her and my brother" Grant said "you guys will never understand what it's like living with a bunch of Halloween grinches".

George and Brian had a look of pity on their faces.

"But anyways enough about me" said Grant "Let's see these costumes". Brian was first, he reached into his black duffle bag and pulled out a skeleton bodysuit. George and Grant faces oozed with amazement due to the fact that last Halloween all Brian had was a simple mask.

George was next, George reached into his black duffle bag and pulled out a sinister reaper costume.

"Now that's what I'm talking about" yelled Grant enthusiastically.

"And check this out" said George. George pulled out a black and silver plastic scythe.

The boys were in pure amazement. It's nothing they loved better than a good Halloween costume.

"If you think that's good check out mine" said Grant.

He pulled out his costume. It's bright eyes and petrifying mask put a smile on the boys' faces.

"Alright let's go ahead and get our costumes on, I want to have enough time to go over the plan one more time so we can all be clear and get ready to leave" grant said anxiously.

Trick-or-Treat

The three boys put on their costumes and gathered around George's table. "Ok so when we leave here we will hit all the houses on this street, it's not the best candy but it will get us started. Then we'll head toward the houses by Dead Man's Forest, that's where the good stuff is at. Then finally we'll all meet back here and go through our candy. Everyone got it?" explained Grant.

"Whoa whoa whoa everything sounded good until you got to the part about Dead Man's Forest, you are crazy if you think I'm going anywhere near there" Brian exclaimed "I don't want anything to do with that place."

"Don't be such a wuss" Grant replied "there is nothing wrong with that forest".

"So your telling me that you would carelessly go by a forest when over 100 people have gone missing in it?" Brian urged.

"What are you talking about" George replied.

"Over the past 3 years over 100 people have gone missing in that forest. Some people say they just got lost and never returned out of it some people say that murderous spirits have been roaming that forest for over 200 years." Brian said with a nervous look on his face.

"Oh c'mon don't tell me you actually believe that crap" Grant insisted "that is just an old kid's myth.

"Ok but don't tell me I didn't tell you so" Brian replied.

The three boys walked out the door with their costumes on and their pillowcases in hand. The dark street was filled with kids running around from door to
door. The only thing that lit up the streets was everyone's porch light.

"Now this what I'm talking about" Grant yelled "Let's Go". The boys ran in the street and joined the other kids.

"This is great" George yelled "It's a lot more people than last year".

The Boys dashed to their first house. The yard of the house was filled with bright Halloween decorations. The three boys ran up to the door and rang the doorbell. Seconds later a women opened the door with a wide smile on her face.

"Trick-or-Treat!" the boys shouted.

The women individually poured candy in the boy's bag.

"Thank you" the boys said as they walked back down the stairs.

"Uh look at this fun size crap" Brian rebuked. "The only thing good about the houses by that stupid forest is that they give out better candy." Brian said.

Speaking of which let's hurry up and hit some more houses on this street so we can go to those houses" Grant replied.

"If you still think I'm going by that forest your crazy" said Brian.

The three boys went to the second house. They walked up the winding pathways and rang the doorbell. Seconds later a man dressed in a werewolf costume came out. "Rarrr !" he screamed. Everyone but Grant jumped.

"Trick-or-Treat...Nice costume" Grant said.

"Thanks" the man replied "would you all like some candy".

"Yes" the boys responded. The man poured the candy into the boys bags and said goodbye.

"Ok let's hit one more house on this street" Grant said. The boys walked to one of the biggest houses on the block. As they walked down the street a boy passed by.

"I wouldn't go to that house if I were you" the boy said "There is a lady who lives there and she is kinda creepy, not the Halloween type creepy but like something wrong with her type creepy."

"We'll take our chances" George said "But thanks".

The boys continued to walk. They soon got to the foot of the steps. The house's yard was filled with tons of life-like Halloween decorations. The boys walked up the elegant stairs to a large brick house. The house had beautiful Halloween colored hanging lights. The boys were in awe. Brian rang the doorbell. A grand chime filled the air. There was no answer. They rang again, seconds later a lady opened the door. Her big grin of missing teeth put a frightened look on the boy's face.

"Trick-or-Treat" Brian said not sure whether to be frightened or joyful.

"Hello little boys" the woman said with her raspy voice "would you all like some candy".

"Uh...sure" Grant said. The woman pulled out a tattered brown bag filled to the top with unwrapped hard candy.

"Umm, on second thought we'll pass" said Grant.

"Please I insist" said the woman. The woman grabbed Grant's bag with her long nailed hands and started to pour.

"Get off!" grant shouted "I said we don't want any". The boys shoved the lady and ran off.

They ran as fast as they could and never looked back. The boys finally came to a stop when they felt to be out of danger. The boys breathed heavily as if they had just sprinted a marathon "We probably should've listened to that boy" said Grant panting.

"You think?" replied George sarcastically.

"That was so weird" George added "What was that ladies deal?"

"I have no clue" Grant replied. "Wait guys" said Bain with a confused look on his face "come to think of it, where the hell are we".

The boys looked around in a circle with a confused look on their face. They were surrounded by tall dark trees with only the moon as a light. The sound of crickets filled the air.

"Why are hell are we in a forest you idiots" shouted George.

"You tell me I was following you" yelled Brian angrily.

"...And I was following Grant" replied George.

The boys turned to Grant shooting hot daggers.

"I was just running; I didn't even notice where I was going." Grant said.

"Wait this place looks familiar" said Brian examining his surroundings. Brian looked at the tall dark trees, the damp mossy ground and then it clicked in his mind.

"Guys I don't think we should be here" said Brian stumbling over his words.

"Why" replied Grant.

"If I am not mistaken this is the exact forest that I was talking about" said Brian with a look as if he had just seen a ghost.

"Wait... this is Dead Man's Forest?" said Grant.

"Shhhh" exclaimed Brian "That is the number one rule about being in this forest. Never Ever say its name out loud".

"How can you believe this crap" shouted Grant. "It's not crap you dummy; this is real" argued Brian.

"I'll prove to you how fake all of this is" said Grant. Grant opened his mouth daring to say the name of the forest aloud.

"Don't do it" screamed Brian "This is not a joke!" Grant continued to mouth the name of the forest daring to say it.

"DEAD... MAN'S.... FORREST!" screamed Grant at the top of his lungs.

The boys were completely still. Quiet came upon them all that could be heard was the crickets of the night.

"WHY WOULD YOU --" Brian said being cut off by a sudden sound.

"What was that" Brian said Stammering over his words.

The boys looked in the direction the sound came from. Suddenly all they could here were footsteps. However, they weren't the footsteps of an animal. They were the footsteps of Brian. The boys turned back to where Brian was standing and all that was left was the imprints of his feet in the damp land.

"Brian!" George and Grant called "Where are you going."

Brian did not reply; He was already too far away. The boys chased after him through the wet dark forest.

"What the heck... why would he just run off" said George.

"I have no clue, he probably got scared" replied Grant.

"Try and call him" said George.

Grant pulled out his cell phone and dialed Brian. The phone rang many times and finally Brian picked up.

"Brian why the hell did you run off" screamed Grant through the cell phone. "I told you not to say it" cried Brian through the phone.

"Nothing even happened, it was just the wind you idiot" said Grant.

"Oh I thought it was the roamer" replied Brian.

"What are you talking about" asked Grant "Who is the roamer".

"You idiots do you not know anything about the history of this town" Brian hollered. "Of course not" said George "Who cares about this town".

"So who is asking for information now you boneheads?" said Brian

"Anyway..." said Brian "two years ago when all those people got taken, the police had one suspect. Sixty five-year-old Roy Jenkins. I know what you guys are thinking why would a sixty five-year-old man be responsible for over one hundred missing people. Well long story short Roy used to live in this forest. He lived all by himself; no family, no kids, no nothing. However, he would always be disturbed by hikers and campers. They would leave trails of garbage all around his house. They ruined his peace or at least that's what he told the police. He got so fed up that one day a group of hikers went into the forest and never returned. It is said to this day that he still roams the forest in search of those and out for vengeance for those who disturbed his home."

"So that's why you have been so afraid of coming into this forest" said Grant.

"Yes don't you get it now" replied Brian.

"Yea ok I guess so just come back so we can go home this night has taken some weird twist and turns. Let's call it a night." said grant sighing.

"Ok" said Brian. "Where are you guys, make a noise so I can find you". "Sure" replied Grant.

"Ok I hear it I'm coming" said Brian.

"Umm, I didn't even make a noise yet" explained Grant. "What do you mean" said Brian "You said you hear something...that something was not us bud" said Grant.

"C'mon Grant stop playing, just stop" said Brian. "I'm not playing with you," said Grant trying to understand Brian "what are you hearing". "Wait so if that wasn't you then who was it" quivered Brian "I don't --" said Grant being cut off by Brian. "Wait shh" whispered Brian. The cellphone became quiet. All that could be heard was the static of the phone.

Static

Static. Static was all Grant heard through the line.

"Brian, Hello" Grant said trying to get Brian back to the phone "Hello are you there Brian?".

"What happened?" asked George watching Grant struggle to hear Brian through the phone. "I don't know; he was saying something but then the line just went quiet" explained Grant. "Let me see" demanded George as if some way he could fix it. Grant handed George the phone. "Hello...Brian...you their buddy?" said George. The line remained quiet. "He's probably playing some dumb joke to get back at us" said Grant. Grant took the phone and pressed end call. "Why would you hang up what if he is in some sort of trouble" Brian urged. "What by the roamer?" Grant mocked "Yeah!" cried George. "Don't tell me your starting to believe in that crap too" said Grant. "I mean you can't lie it sounded a little believable" replied George.

"Not by a long shot" said Grant. "Whatever, let's just go find him" replied George. "Brian" yelled Grant through the echoing forest. "Where are you" George yelled. The boys searched for a little over 5 minutes but had no luck. All of a sudden the phone rang. The sudden tone frightened the boys.

"Who is it?" asked George. Brian pulled out his phone and the bright screen read "Brian". "It's Brian" Grant exclaimed.

"Answer it" yelled George. Brian answered the phone. "Hello, Hello Brian you there" Grant said trying to get a reply. There was no answer. All that could be heard was the static over the airways.

Grant tried again. "Brian, C'mon stop playing this is not funny anymore, I 'm cold and ready to get out of this damn forest" yelled Grant into the microphone of his phone. There was no reply again. Suddenly Grant began to hear something coming out of the phone and this time it wasn't just static.

The mysterious sound began to get louder and louder. It sounded as if someone was trudging over dead leaves. Grant put the phone back up to his face. "Brian is that you?" Grant said desperately through the phone.

"Guys he coming" Brian croaked through the phone. "Brian who's coming" fretted Grant.

"It's him -- it's Roy" shrieked Brian "he's here...Run while you still...".

Brian's voice cut off. All of a sudden a sound came out of the phone. It wasn't just any sound. This sound put a feeling of dread down your spine. The sound coming out of the phone was unbearably loud. So loud Grant had to remove the phone away from his face. So loud George could hear it through the phone. It was Brian. The screams of his cold, fearful, shivering body could be heard throughout the forest as well as through the phone.

The boys had no clue what was going on. They ran toward the noise. "Brian" Grant shouted through the forest. "Brian" shouted George. They got not reply. They screamed Brian's name countless times but got no reply.

Finally, they stopped running because they could barely feel their legs. The boys panted heavily. Grant pressed the phone back up to his face to try and reach Brian, but he had no luck. Suddenly, the sound of breathing came from the phone.

The breath was cold and steady. It was like it could be felt on Grant's neck through the phone.

"Oh thank god" Grant said relieved to hear Brian through the phone. "I knew you were playing some kind of practical joke, you had us out here thinking you were actually in some kind of trouble" Grant said.

The line was silent and staticy. The breathing continued. "So are you going to say something or just let me listen to you breathing the whole time" said Grant jokingly "Brian you there?".

The breathing got louder and louder. Grant felt as if the cold breath of the person behind the phone was right on his neck. Slowly but surely he began to realize that the person behind the cellphone was not who he thought it was. Grant has known Brian for over 5 years and he knew...that was no Brian.

Grant walked over to George and put the phone on speaker so he could hear. "I don't think this is Brian" Grant whispered to George.

"Mute the phone" George mouthed. Grant muted the phone. "I don't know man this is so weird; I was talking on the phone to who I thought was Brian but all I hear is heavy breathing" Grant rambled.

"Slow down, slow down!" George said trying to calm down Grant "Let me see the phone". Grant handed George the phone. "Hello, who is this" said George. The breathing continued "I said WHO IS THIS!" yelled George. "You damn people just won't leave me alone will you?" the man hissed evilly. " Wh-who is this" George stuttered. George put the phone on speaker phone so Grant could hear him. "Whoever this is you need to tell us right now where our friend is" demanded Grant.

"You should have listen to your friend" he said in a raspy voice. Grant and George were stunned with a face of terror on their face. Suddenly all they hear is a muffled voice over the phone. "Brian and George run before it's too - "Brian could barely get the last word out before the only thing Grant and George heard was the dial tone of the phone. "BRIANNNN" screamed George. "This cannot be happening" George wept.

"This can't be real" exclaimed Grant "He probably just pranking us. "Think about it, He got mad that we weren't gullible enough to fall for his dumb horror story.

Grant said putting air quotes on the word "horror". "So he put on this whole act to prove us wrong and make us look like idiots.

"Grant wake the hell up why would he do that, one of our best friend has been taken and in trouble by some guy and your standing there still trying to find a way to protect your ego. I'm done with this I am going to find him and bring him back safely with or without you." George said walking off. "George wait!" said Grant catching back up to him. "I'm sorry for being so insensitive" grant apologized.

"..." George stayed silent.

"I care for Brian just as much as you do" said. Nothing but silence came from George.

"Are you really going to ignore me this whole time" asked Grant. "This WHOLE night all you have done is treated George like he's not one of your best friends" George said, "This whole night all you have done is shot him down... he tried to tell us about the forest; you didn't listen and now where is he, where is he-- oh yeah, GONE. Grant fell silent.

Brian and George trotted through the wet leaves of the forest with nothing but awkward feelings toward each other and thought of finding Brian.

"Where do you think he could be?" asked Grant.

George shrugged his shoulders "Look I'm sorry about how I have been acting but can we please just put this behind us and try to find Brian, It's getting really late and there is no way we can go back home without him.

The boys walked for what felt like miles and suddenly the two boys stumbled into a strange print in the wet, muddy leaves. "George come check this out" called Grant.

Grant examined the print. "You think this is George's footprint".

"It has to be who else comes out here" said George.

"Well if there is one then there is probably more" replied Grant.

The boys moved on from the footprint and moved on. Suddenly another one followed on after it. The boys suddenly began following trail of human footprints.

"We must be getting closer" said George relieved. The boys followed the footprints.

"Hey I'm sorry for freaking out" said George "I just don't want to see anything to happen to Brian".

"I understand, you were right for it, I was being a jerk and you helped me realize it so I'm sorry too" apologized Grant.

The boys continued to walk along the footprint trail and all of a sudden the path came to an end.

" That's weird" said George, "The trail ends here but there's no sign of Brian."

The boys began to walk around and examine their surroundings. All that surrounded them was the wet cold leaves and the previous footprints of Brian.

Gone

The two boys searched for what felt like hours. However, no trace of Brian could be found.

"How is this even possible" George said "We were following his footprints and all of a sudden they just come to an end."

The boys stood still with a puzzled look on their face. They were at a loss for words.

"Maybe we should look around for traces of him" suggested Grant.

"Good Idea" replied George.

The two boys split up and looked around for any trace of where Brian could be.

"Where could he be" Grant thought to himself as he flipped over a large rock. Grant sighed.

He began walking back through the forest checking things such as matted down leaves to the insides of puddles but there was still no sign of Brian.

He began to walk back to where George was searching. However, all of a sudden something caught his eye. Grant couldn't make out what it was. He began walking closer and closer to it to see what it was. Suddenly, it began clear to him that it was a house. "What the hell" Grant said to himself. "George !!" Grant called back. After the sound of Grant voice cleared, the forest stayed silent Grant began to inch closer and closer to the house. The house was covered in darkness as if it were hiding in the shadows of the gnarled old trees that surrounded it. It appeared to be stained with the color of a house that suffered a severe fire. The windows were boarded up with wood and the ones that weren't boarded up were shattered leaving only sharp shards. The black sloping roof of the house appeared to be tilting over. Grant's brain and logical reason was telling him to go back and check in with George but his curiosity was telling him otherwise.

He stepped on the first step of the house and a loud creak echoed through the forest. Then, he walked up the remaining steps up to the front door. The numbers next to the front door read "0611" He peeked inside through the cracks in the boarded up windows. Inside, the house appeared to be abandoned. There was only old dusty furniture and tattered wallpaper that bordered the walls.

Grant began to further examine the house. "I wonder if Brian passed through here", he thought. He walked around to the back of the house. The same dreary and frightening exterior continued. However, this time there was what looked to be an underground cellar on the side of the house.

The cellar was surrounded by grass poking through the dead leaves on the ground. Grant approached it with an uneasy look on his face. The rusted cellar doors were tightly chained shut with some sort of lock.

Grant got on his knees and further examined the cellar doors. The doors were coated with brown rust and one of the cellar door handles was on the brink of falling off. The numbers on the rusty old padlock read the scrambled numbers "8621". Grant began to input random numbers into the padlock.

"3...4...5..8" Grant pulled at the lock however it didn't budge.

"1...2...7...3" Grant pulled at the lock again. "Nope"

Grant was relieved that the cellar was locked but at the same time he was slightly disappointed that his curiosity high had come to an end. He got up and began to exit the area of the house.

"I wonder how long this house has been here" Grant thought to himself walking away.

"More importantly who is crazy enough to live in the middle of the woods".

As grant continued to walk away he turned back and took one long look at the house. He stared at every detail of the house: the boarded up windows, the shattered windows, the tar colored exterior, suddenly Grant eyes wandered over the numbers next to the front door. The numbers read "0611" suddenly Grant's curiosity peaked again.

He wanted to try one more time just for the sake of it. Grant walked back to the back of the house where the cellar was located. He got on his knees and took the padlock in his hand." Why am I doing this" Grant thought "Who knows what could be down here" Contradictory of his previous thoughts Grant began to flip the numbers of the padlock.

0...6...1...1...*SNAP*

Unlocking of the lock frightened Grant. He couldn't believe that the number combination worked. Grant slid the chains off the door, still in disbelief. He could not believe what he was about to do.

Grant took a deep look around himself and seconds later opened one of the doors. The old rusted doors rotated open and it was so dark that it appeared to be another black sheet in place where the door was. Grant's face began to resemble what it would look like if he was at the top of a hill on a rollercoaster. As he took in the view of the black abyss, he attempted to adjust his eyes and see what lay in the dark however, in his eyes the inside stayed dark.

Grant knew there was no way he was going down there with it being as dark as it was. Suddenly, Grant remembered the flashlight that he packed in his bag. He took his book bag of his back and took his flashlight out. "This better work" said to himself. Grant flipped the switch of the flashlight...The bulb of the flashlight illuminated the stairs of the dark underground room.

Hello" Grant yelled into the tunnel with a frightened voice.

The slightly illuminated room stayed quiet. Grant took the first step into the dark room.

"Hello" Grant repeated again.
The room remained quiet. He took another step into the underground.

"Hello" Grant repeated for a third time.

The silence of the room struck Grant for a third time. This time Grant stepped down the last 2 steps.

Grant flashed the light and illuminated the underground cellar. The old brick room was filled with dirt on the ground and cobwebs in the corner of the walls. He had a feeling that that wasn't the only room apart of the underground. "What kind of underground cellar is this" he thought to himself.

Grant looked around the cellar. Three dark hallways stood in front of him. Terror was starting to rise inside of him. He knew that he didn't belong down there but he was.

He flashed the depth of all 3 hallways; none of them were the same length. One was very short the second one was slightly longer than the first but the last one... he knew there was no way he would be going down there.

Grant began to pace down the first hallway. "Ugh, what is that smell" he said putting his hands over his nose. The hallway had a peculiar smell to it. It was indescribable. It was almost like someone had died, had been locked in a box, rotted and someone else opened the box.

As he kept walking, the pattern on the walls stayed the same for the first couple of steps. However, as Grant kept walking down the dark hallway he began to notice a change in the features. He began to see what he assumed were prison-like walls.

Grant flashed the light to the bordering wall. It wasn't just a wall. It was exactly what he thought...a cell door. He turned and faced the front of the cell door. Through the bars, he gazed upon the interior of the prison cell. In the corner of the tight boxy cell stood a dirty steel toilet.

"Gross" he screamed. Against the wall, across from the dirty toilet, was a steel bed frame with a plastic mattress on top of it. Grant stood with a puzzled look on his face.

"What house has a prison under it?" Grant thought to himself. As he began to walk away from the prison cell, the original smell began to get stronger and stronger.

Seconds later, another prison cell came into the view. Grant stopped in his tracks as the smell coming from in front of him was becoming too much to handle.

"Oh my God" Grant said putting his shirt over his nose.

Grant started to take small steps closer and closer to the cell in front of him. Seconds later Grant was face front with the second prison cell of the hallway. However, there was something different about this one. The bars were rusted, the cell was smaller and there was no toilet or bed and the cell was open, but also there was something in the corner of the cell where the toilet was...a mysterious bag that had Grant guessing.

Grant attempted to get a better view of the bag through the bars of the cell, however, they were restricting. He took a deep breath, trying not to breathe through his nose, then crept inside the cell. The old cell door squealed open as he went in. The smell only got stronger as he approached the bag in the corner. Inching closer and closer, soon he was standing over the source of the smell that had been aerating through the underground.

Grant bent down and slowly slid the bag closer toward himself. Slowly he opened it and almost immediately the smell of dead and rotten flesh was amplified. Seconds later all that could be heard were loud footsteps. The footsteps weren't getting closer they were getting farther from where Grant was standing, but it's not what you are thinking. These weren't the footsteps of another person...these were the footsteps of Grant... he was gone.

Gone like the sun on the strike of the day's eve. Running from whatever drove terror so deep into the soul of his body that he felt the need to do so. He had no clue what it was but all he knew was that he didn't belong down there and he had to get out fast. Grant sprinted all the way from the cell that he was in to the exit of the underground cellar with nothing in mind but escaping.

Author's Note

Carrington was inspired by predictable horror movies. His aim was to make the book unpredictable and keep the readers on their toes.

Fun Fact

Although he has only played it for 3 years, basketball is one of Carrington's favorite sports. He has also played soccer, golf and baseball.

Emergence

Grant emerged from the underground cellar gasping for air and trying to catch his breath. He huffed and puffed just to get a slightest breath of air. His face was frozen with a look of confusion, fear, and disgust.

"What the hell was that?", he thought. "What could that have been? Who is so sick and vile to have prison cells in an underground cellar with dead rotting flesh and shackles?", Grant said to himself as he tried to recover. "I thought this house was surely abandoned".

Attempting to rap his mind around what just happened, Grant heard something beside him. He froze in place; trying to hear and also see what it was. It could have been the wind, or a tree hitting up against something. Whatever it was had startled Grant enough to put him in a full defensive position. It could have been nothing, but being that he had just ran out of a mysterious underground cellar filled with rotting flesh, prison cells and shackles, anything could happen!

The sound in the forest got louder and louder as something was getting closer and closer. Seconds later, a little animal popped out of the bushes. It appeared to be a chipmunk. However, no matter how adorable the chipmunk was Grant's mind was still filled with questions, his mind was still racing with allegations and theories about the previous events.

"What if Brian was right...what if Dead Man's Forest really is haunted?"

"What if Roy Jenkins really is out for vengeance?"

"What if... Wait...GEORGE !!!"

All this time Grant was supposed to be looking for traces of Brian. Unfortunately, he has been screwing around exploring old abandoned houses and their underground cellars while one of his best friends was stuck in a forest. Alone, looking for someone. Grant knew he had messed up. He took off to try and find him before it was too late.

"GEORGE !?" Grant screamed through the forest cutting through bushes and splashing u water from the wet, damp leaves.

Grant felt a sharp pain in the depths of his abdomen. It wasn't like any other pain. It wasn't the type of pain that tells you that you needed to use the bathroom or the one you have when sitting next to a trash can with your head in it. It was something more like a feeling. It was guilt. The guilt that he had put on himself because of his poor judgement and decision making. He knew that if he had lost both of his friends in one night due to something he caused, he would not be able to live with himself.

Grant continued to sprint through the dark forest. Screaming George's name step by step.

"George!"

"George !! where are you ?!" Grant's pace began to get slower and slower eventually he was at a slow walking pace. He knew he needed to keep running but at the same time his legs were too tired to continue. Grant huffed and puffed as he continued to walk screaming George's name.

"George!......George!?" He began to recognize the area surrounding him and remembered when he ventured off from George. Suddenly, as he walked around a large tree. A body collided with his. Frightened, Grant jumped with a fearful look on his face. To his pleasant surprise there stood George, holding the area of his head where the two bumped.

Although George was feeling pain, he was feeling so many more emotions than that; including anger and fear. "George, you have no idea how happy I am to see you, but there is no time for that we need to..." George interrupted him, "Save it, I can't believe you, instead of looking for the main PRIORITY - Brian. I have spent the past 45 minutes looking for your butt" he   yelled.

"George we need to..." "Shut up, I'm not done" George said cutting off Grant.

"...Wandering if I am going to ever see my two so called best friends ever again. You know what SCREW YOU Grant. I'm done with you. This whole night you have put yourself before

51

everybody. "Find Brian and yourself out of the forest yourself". George said immediately storming off.

"George wait you don't understand we need to get out of here like now!" said Grant as he watched George storm off in a huff."

"Why what do you have to say now, I'm..." said George being cut off by Grant.

"When I was out looking for Brian I noticed a HOUSE deep into the woods" said Grant.

"What are you talking about" questioned George.

"Shh now is not the time for questions just LISTEN!", exclaimed Grant

"I walked around the house and at the back of it and it had this underground cellar" Grant explained.

"Ok and what" George said as he still questioned Grant.

Grant continued to explain "And there was a padlock so I started trying combinations for some reason I don't even know why. But none of them worked so I just left. But then when I was leaving for some reason I just felt the need to try one last time. I saw the address number on the door so I went back and tried it, and... It opened. But there is really no time to explain anymore we need to go like NOW!"

"And just leave Brian out in the forest?" said George.

"I'm sorry but at this point we just need to." Grant started to say until being cut off from the sound of something.

"What was that?"

"What was what" said George.

"We need to go NOW!" yelled Grant.

"Grant what the hell are you..."

Suddenly a man shot out of the bushes. The boys jumped in fear. The masked man was wielding a silver knife.

"George look out !!!" Grant said shoving George out of the way. George gasped and the boys immediately took off in one direction. They had no idea which way they were going but hoped they would find an end to the forest.

"WHO WAS THAT!" Grant said running through the forest as tree branches smacked him in the face.

"I don't know, keep running!! "George said

"Actually I think I'll stop and introduce myself to the masked killer with a knife trying to murder us. "Grant responded.

"Do you think this is a joke" George yelled to Grant, continuing to sprint through the forest. You must think this whole thing is just a big JOKE"

Grant remained quiet as he sprinted through the forest. He wanted to believe George was still by his side but fear would not allow him to look and be sure.

Authors Note

This book was published in April of 2019.

Fun Fact

Carrington has one sibling who is in college in New York.

Headlights

As Grant and George ran through the forest, Grant began to notice a gleam of light that looked like what could've been a street light.

"George do you see that" Grant said as they began to stop thinking they were in the clear "Follow that light".

The two turned toward the light; not knowing whether the light meant safety or not. As they got closer and closer they began to realize it more and more what it was. Sadly, it wasn't another street light. The boys emerged into the street   an   immediately

...HONK   ...   SCREECHH   ...

George gasped and froze like a deer in headlights. While Grant immediately jumped out of the way. Grant could see the situations unfold as if it was in slow motion, however he knew that nothing could be done at that point.

...CRASHHH

The car immediately pressed on the brakes but it was too late. Grant could not believe what he had just seen. How one night could go so badly. How did what should have been one of the best nights of the year most likely be one of the worst.

"GEORGEEE" yelled Grant.

George laid in silence as blood ran from his head.

"GEORGE!" yelled Grant again.

The person stepped outside of the smashed car. "OH MY GOD!" he screamed.

The person that stepped out of the car was a man wearing a black suit with a red tie.

"Is he ok?" the man said as he ran over to George.

"Call 911!" yelled Grant

The man pulled out his phone from the back of his suit pants and dialed 911. "There has been an accident! we need an ambulance at…" the man paused and looked around for a street name. However, the street was just one long road outlined with trees.

"Sir has anyone been hurt?" The responder asked

"Yes, two boys were involved, and one is not responsive" he said.

"Sir we are sending an ambulance to your location now" the responder said finally.

After the man got off the phone he immediately ran over to George. Grant sat by his side trying to get a response from him.

"What were you to boys doing in the street like that" The man said as he stood by George with a worried look on his face. "I know this is going to sound weird" Grant said getting ready to explain "but we were being chased by some man and I don't know why. We were trying to get out of the forest so we just ran in one direction.

"So you're telling me that some man was chasing you in the middle of the night" suddenly the man looked over to his watch "I'm sorry...The morning in the forest".

Suddenly before Grant could respond, the sound of an ambulance filled the surrounding area.

"Finally" Grant said as he got up and waved the ambulance down as they progressed down the long road.

As the ambulance inched closer and closer to the scene Grant realized the actuality of what just happened and it got more and more surreal. Grant could not believe all the events that unfolded that night and he could only think that it was all his fault. When the ambulance finally pulled up the red, white and blue lights began to blind Grant. The paramedics got out of the truck immediately and pulled out the gurney. Grant had never seen what actually happens when stuff like this happens. The paramedics ran over to were George lay with the gurney and began to do what paramedics do.

"What are you two boys doing out here this late at night" one of the paramedics asked.
Grant remained quiet as the paramedics continued to do their work. Minutes later what sounded like another ambulance started to come down the street. Suddenly Grant began to realize that it was a bit different from the ambulance siren. As the car inched closer and closer, the

blue and red lights revealed the car to be a police car.

As the police car pulled up Grant began to get extremely nervous. When the police car pulled up a white police officer got out the car. Grant had fear all over his face as the police walked over to him.

"I need you to explain to me what happened hear son "the police officer said to Grant.

Grant looked over to George as the paramedics worked to get George in the ambulance. "Well sir... me and my friend George were in the forest looking for someone but a man came out of nowhere and began to chase us.

The police officer looked into Grant's eyes as if he was crazy.

"Ok son do you have a parent's number that I can get in contact with?"

Grant had no idea what the police officer was saying, he was only focused on what was going on with George. He glanced back over to George and saw him being loaded in the ambulance.

"Son what is your parents' contact information?" asked the police officer again.

"I... I don't know Grant said. A tear began to run down the side of his cheek as he saw the ambulance   pull   off. The police officer sighed "Do you have your parents' address memorized so that I can take you there?"

Grant wiped the tears off the side of his cheek "Um...yes I think so"
"Ok go wait in the back of the car" the police officer said. He walked to the black police cruiser with his shoulders hanging. He had no clue how he was going to explain this to his family. Grant opened the door of the police car, he had never been in a police car and never had expected him to be in one either.

Grant said down reluctantly. The seat was hard, black and cold. Grant felt a cold shiver on his body. He sat in the police car and waited for the officer to get in.

Two minutes later the officer opened the door and got in the cruiser.

"What's the address son?" the officer asked Grant as he locked his eyes on Grant through the rearview mirror.

Grant wiped his face again from the past tears "3125 Elaine Court" Grant said.

The police put his seatbelt on and took off from the scene. Grant turned towards the window and got lost in his thoughts.

Author's Note

It took Carrington 7 months to write this book.

Fun Fact

Carrington aspires to be an engineer when he grows up.

The Storm

W ake up, we're here" The officer said

the front seat. "Grant slowly rose leaving a puddle of drool on the arm rest and even more on his face. He had no clue what was to come once he got out of that police car. How would his brother react? More importantly how would his mother react. Just the thought of it made Grant terrified. A storm was coming and he knew it.

The officer got out of the car and walked around to Grant's door. Grant stood still in the car thinking about what was to come as the officer opened the car door. Grant stepped out of the car next to the officer.

"This is your house right?" the officer asked. "Yes sir" Grant said quietly.

Grant and the officer began to walk toward the house. Grant began to get even more nervous he had no clue how we would explain everything to his mom. The officer and Grant reached the front door. Reality stood right in front of Grant and took a long gaze into his eyes.

"Well ring the doorbell" said the officer. Grant looked at the doorbell and took a gulp of fear. The officer waited impatiently for him to scurry up the confidence to ring the doorbell. Grant sighed.

DINNGGG DOONNNGGG

Grant and the officer stood at the door waiting for someone to come door. The officer looked down at Grant while Grant stood dead still and looked straight.

"I just have one question son." the officer said.

Grant stayed silent.

"Why on Earth were you boys out there that late at night?"

Grant sighed and remained silent. Suddenly the door creaked open. Grant's head slowly dropped and all he could look at was his shoes. As the door open wider and wider a woman began to appear in the doorway.

"GRANT WINSLOW GREEN where the hell have you been. You have had your me and not to mention your brother worried sick about you. I sent you out to have a good time with your friends and 10 hours later you come back with a police officer! Someone needs to explain what's going on right NOW."

Ma'am your son has been involved in a missing persons case and has been responsible for a young boy who has been injured. We don't know the severity of it yet.... from what he tells me he was struck by a moving vehicle. This is all I know now but your son will be required to come in for questioning at a later hour this week. I just wanted to let you know what's going on.

Grant's mother took a deep breath and tried to wrap her head around what the police officer just said.

"I apologize if I haven't formally introduced myself, my name is Officer Diggs." said the officer.

"Thank you officer, I am so sorry for the trouble my son has caused you" Grant's mom said peering over to Grant. His eyes were stuck to his shoes.

"You are very welcome if there's anything else I can do to you can reach me by calling the

Thomasville Police Station and just ask for Officer Diggs" The officer said as he got ready to leave.

"Ok have a good night Officer Diggs" Grant's mom said. "As for you, young man, get in that house!" Grant sped into the house and said nothing. His mother followed and slammed the door behind her.

Grant attempted to make it up the stairs before he had to hear his mother's yells but it was too late. "I don't know what came over you tonight that made you think that was ok to sneak out of the house and go with your friends when I blatantly said that we had something else planned." Grant's mother hissed.

Grant remained silent and took it because he knew that nothing could be said to get out of what he did.

"I don't think you understand how worried you had your brother and me." she continued.

"What do you have to say for yourself" Grant's mother said, trying to hold her composure.

Grant took a deep breath and got ready to explain the scariest, saddest, and most regretful night he had lived through.

"So… It started this evening after you told me that I couldn't go trick or treating with Brian and George. You said we had something else to do, but you know how I love doing this with them every year. I went upstairs, got my stuff, and jumped out of the window using tied up sheets. I immediately took off for George's house. I knew it was wrong, but I did it anyway. Once everyone got to George's house we put on our Halloween costumes and went trick-or-treating. Things started to get weird when we got to this one house. There was an old lady and she was trying to grab us. We ran away from her and didn't look back. All of a sudden we realized that we had run into a forest."

As Grant tried to continue to explain the sound of his mother's phone came from the kitchen. "This is not over" she mother said to him. As she walked into the kitchen, Grant saw his chance and snuck off to his room.

Grant creeped up the creaking stairs, entered his room and shut the door. "How could this night get any worse" Grant said. His mind began to race with hypothetical questions …

"What if I go to jail?"

"What if the kids at school find out?"

"What if I get in any more trouble with mom?"

"What if they find out about..."

Grant peered over to the alarm clock on his dresser it read "3:56". He tried to slow his racing mind and attempt to get some sleep before school in the morning. He laid on his bed and closed his eyes.

Author's Note

This book was written for a school assignment. When Carrington first heard he had to write a book for his 10th grade literature class he was planning to write a historical fiction book about the story of a slave.

Fun Fact

Carrington's favorite subject in school is science. He enjoys how broad the subject is and how you can never know everything about science.

Eyes

BEEP...BEEP...BEEP...BEEP

Grant arose to the sound of his alarm clock. He turned over to it and turned it off. The clock read 7:45 AM; there were 15 minutes before he had to go to school and he was not ready for what he knew he was going to have to face...speculations and accusations all throughout the day.

Grant got out of bed and walked up to his dresser mirror. He stood there looking at himself as his mind raced. He sighed and walked out of his room. As he walked to his bathroom he passed his brothers room.

"Good morning Grant" his little brother JJ said, unaware of what happened the previous night.

Grant ignored him and kept walking. He reached his bathroom and closed the door. Then, he turned on the steaming shower and did his normal morning routine; just like it was any other day. He knew it wasn't.

As Grant finished getting ready for school he noticed something that he had never noticed before. In his house, there was a strange silence. He did not hear the sizzling of his mother's morning bacon. He did not hear his brother's favorite morning show. He did not hear his neighbor's dogs barking at the mailman. There was only silence. Grant finished tying his shoes and headed downstairs. When he got downstairs he was surprised to see his mother sitting at the dining table.

"Good morning mom", he said not knowing what kind of mood to expect from his mother.

She sat there quietly ignoring the sound of Grant's voice.

Grant sighed and walked into the kitchen. When he got to the kitchen he was not surprised when he didn't see any breakfast made for him. He checked the cabinets for some toast but there was none; He checked the refrigerator for juice but all that was left was an empty bottle of "V-9 Splash". Not seeing any food or drinks he could possibly have before school, he picked up his bag and headed for the door. Suddenly his mother interrupted him as he was heading for the door.

"I will pick you up from school at 4 PM sharp" she said. "The detective wants to see you today...don't make me wait."

"Ok" he said "Bye".

Grant's mother sat in silence as he walked out the door.

As he closed the door, Grant walked down his outside stairs and headed to the bus stop. As he was walking he began to think about all the possible things kids would speculate. The more and more he thought about it the more and more his stomach turned.

As he arrived at his bus stop he checked the time and wondered why his bus had not arrived yet. In his mind he thought of it as a blessing in disguise because he knew it was more time that he would not have to face what he knew was coming.

Waiting for his bus Grant sat on a nearby bench. As he sat there, the night before we played over and over again in his mind. That exact moment when he saw the blinding headlights and how they inched closer and closer to George's body. It replayed in slow motion but in reality it happened at the speed of light.

Grant's mind soon shifted to the well-being of George. He was clueless about his condition and he could only expect the worse. The more Grant thought about George; the more he wanted to take out his phone and call him.

Grant thoughts were soon interrupted by the screeching of the school bus wheels.

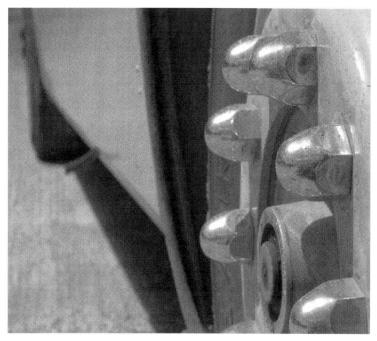

Grant sighed and grabbed his bag to get on to the school bus. He could hear the rowdy children from the bench. As he approached the school bus the noise became louder and louder. Grant stepped up each stair of the bus knowing that with each step he was closer to hell.

"Could you move any slower" the bus driver hissed at Grant with a nasty attitude.

"Oh I-I'm sorry ma'am" Grant stuttered back.

"Just hurry up kid" she said, agitated.

As Grant walked down the aisle of the bus he kept his head and eyes straight and tried to avoid any eye contact with the kids on the bus. What Grant saw was the back emergency door of the bus, but what the kids saw was a weird kid that was involved in an investigation the previous night.

Grant walked straight to the back of the bus where he found an empty seat.

He plopped down; relieved that no one had made a big scene or started asking questions yet.

Grant knew he had spoken too soon as a young girl who seemed to be in a grade below him turned around. From the seat in front of him, she looked him dead in the eyes.

Are you that boy that got lost in the woods with his friends? She asked.

Grant sighed and palmed his face because he knew that the start of a long day had begun.

"So are you?" the girl repeated. "It wasn't like that" Grant finally said to the girl.

"Well what do you mean" she replied

"Look, I really don't want to talk about this" Grant said to the girl. Her questions aggravated him.

The girl turned around in her seat; facing forward and continued doing what she was doing. Grant as he sat back in his seat and waited to get to school.

Grant had felt the first taste of questioning. It was not pleasant but he realized that if he just shut down the questioner before they could ask their questions then he could survive.

As minutes past, Grant had noticed that he was getting closer and closer to the school.

Eventually they arrived right in front of the school. Grant was overwhelmed as he saw countless amounts of students walk into the doors of the school. It felt like he had not been in an environment like this in weeks.

As all the kids unloaded the bus Grant was left sitting there still trying to get his mind right to go inside the school.

"Kid again with this get off my bus" driver yelled at Grant again.

He looked out the window of the bus and back to the bus driver. He knew he was going to have to eventually get off the bus.

Grant picked up his book bag, walked down the aisle of the bus, and stepped off. Once he began walking to the school he felt as if everyone's eyes were stuck on him and he just couldn't shake them off. For every step he took the more eyes he felt on him.

Entering the school, he was immediately overwhelmed by all the commotion.

"Hey Grant!" a girl said walking up to him.

Grant almost jumped out of his shoes, startled to hear a voice directed toward him. He never expected someone to walk up and start a conversation on a weird day like this.

"Whoa...you ok" the girl said to a surprised Grant.

"Yeah I'm ok...why wouldn't I be" he replied.

"Geez, I'm just asking, weirdo!" the girl said as she ran off.

RINGGGG

All the students flooded out of the hallway as the sound of the bell echoed through the halls of the school.

"Grant put his hand in his face and walked to class."

His first class was English is most dreaded subject in school. Grant walked through the doors of his class and straight to his seat.

"Good morning class, how are you all today?" Ms. Dell the English energetically said to the class.

However, the class remained silent.

Ms. Dell stood without saying anything; waiting for a response from the students.

"Well alright then, today's Do Now: write 4-5 sentences stating how and why your Halloween was good and bad." Ms. Dell said reading off the board. "You will have 10 minutes and then we will share out."

Grant sighed and took out a piece of paper. As Grant took out a piece of paper he prayed that the teacher wouldn't look at him to read his.

Grant placed the paper on his desk looking at it. He knew that he couldn't write what he really did for Halloween, but he had to write something. Time passed and five minutes in Grant had nothing on his paper but his name.

"You have five more minutes left" the teacher said to the class.

Grant began to panic, trying to think of what to write. He picked up his pencil "For Halloween I stayed home" he wrote".

"And that is time" the teacher said to the class "pencils down"

Grant exhaled in a relief that he was able to get something down on his paper.
"Would anybody like to volunteer to present first?" the teacher asked the class

The class remained so silent a pen could be heard drop on the floor; They looked at the teacher like a deer in headlights.

"Well alright... Amy would you like to present?" Ms. Dell asked he star student

"I would love to" Amy said popping up out of her seat with a smug look on her face.

She walked up front and center to the classroom voluntarily and cleared her throat.

"For Halloween this year I went Trick-or-Treating all around my neighborhood, it was a good Halloween because I got a lot of candy"

"Very good Amy" Ms. Dell said as she was the only one clapping

Ms. Dell looked around the classroom for someone else to present. Grant ducked his head behind the girl sitting in front of him as Ms. Dell's eyes wandered to his side of the room.

"Grant I would like to hear from" Ms. Dell said

Grant sunk in his chair because he knew he would have to lie about his Halloween.

"Ms. Dell do I have to?"

"If you want your points for today Grant"

The kids in the back of the class snickered. Grant resentfully walked up to the front of the room. He tried to avoid noticing the kids in the room but he knew it was going to be hard if he began to talk.

"For Halloween this year I... I" grant tried to get his words out but they wouldn't budge.
The kids in the audience began to snicker obnoxiously.

"For Halloween I just stayed inside" Grant finally said.

"That's not what I heard" a muffled voice said from the back of the classroom.
The crowd burst out into laughter as Grant ran out of the room embarrassed.

As Grant ran down the hallway with tears falling down his eyes, the pain in his heart increased. The feeling of guilt was almost overwhelming! He now knew that everyone in the school was aware of what happened the previous night and that was not something he thought he could live with.

As Grant ran down the hallway he looked for somewhere to go where he could escape to. Grant finally found a vacant room to go to. Grant walked into the dark room and gathered himself. He tried to flip the light switch but it didn't work. How was he going to continue the day with this lingering in the air? The dark room brought him back to the previous night. The more he stayed in the room the more he began to remember. Grant knew he could not stay in the room for any longer. As Grant began to walk out of the room he saw a dark figure in the corner of the room. The slender frame filled up the space in the corner. Grant's heartbeat rose rapidly. Grant did not stay in the room for any longer. He sprinted out just as he sprinted out previously.

As he left the room the sound of the bell entered the hallways. It was time for lunch. He did not know what was going to happen; he knew, however, the only way to get through the rest of the day was to get through lunch.

As Grant began to walk to the lunchroom he was on high alert for anyone coming to say something to him.

He entered the large room feeling overwhelmed. It was as if he had not entered the exact same room thousands of times.

"What's up Grant" a boy said walking past him smiling.

Grant remained silent as the boy passed.

Grant walked to the lunch line, keeping his head down. He filled his tray with the usual cafeteria slop and walked out of line. He stopped to find an open seat away from a lot of people.

He headed to an open seat in the corner of the cafeteria. He walked quickly so he could hurry and sit down without anyone noticing his face.

Sitting down, he began to do as he did on any other normal day. Inside he hoped that no one would approach him.

Sadly, his hope was crushed as a group of kids headed straight to his table. As he noticed the group approaching he tried to hide his face.

"Are you Grant?" one kid asked.

Grant remained quiet.

The kids began to giggle at Grant's silence.

"Did you hear me?", the kid asked.

"Yes" Grant mumbled; his voice remaining very low.

"You want to tell us what happened last night" The boy said "I heard you killed your best friend"

"T-That's not true" Grant said hesitantly.

The crowd walked away satisfied, thinking that they got to Grant.

Lunch time sped by and Grant was happy it was over. The bell rang and Grant got his book bag and sped out the cafeteria.

One more class for the day and he would be done having to watch over his shoulder and be on the lookout for obnoxious middle schoolers.

Grant headed to his last period. Science this was his favorite subject and he hoped that it would help him get to the end of the day. Grant entered the classroom and did not see his normal teacher. The substitute sat at the teacher's desk was uninterested and on her phone.

Grant sighed. He didn't walk to his normal desk. Instead he took a desk in the back. The problem was that this was where all the not so good kids sit. Grant getting questioned and picked on was inevitable. As he sat down the rest of the class flooded in and filled the seats. Per usual the not so good kids headed to the back and the kids who did all their work sat in the front.

"Ok everyone, my name is Ms. Mac, I will be your substitute today." she said with a southern accent. "Your teacher didn't leave any work, so you can do whatever; just don't be loud." The kids' faces lit up with smiles except for Grant. He put his head down on his desk in the back corner of the classroom while all the kids began to chat.

As Grant closed his eyes he began to see people in the dark empty space. He couldn't make out who they were but he knew it wasn't good that he was seeing them. Time passed and suddenly the school bell rang. Grant had no idea where the time had gone but he was glad that it had passed. When Grant lifted his head up the classroom was empty. The desks were scattered everywhere, paper was on the floor and it looked as if a tornado had gone through the class.

Grant got his book bag, got up from the desk and walked out the classroom. The halls were empty just like the classroom. Grant turned a corner and there he was! George was standing right in front of him.

"George!?" Grant called out!

Grant squinted his eyes trying to verify that it was who he thought it was.

Suddenly a loud voice filled the hallway.

"Grant! .... Grant!! .... GRANT!!!"

Suddenly, Grant awoke his head shot straight into the air as the light of the classroom entered his eyes.

Ms. Mac stood over Grant as he noticed the empty class.

"It's time to go home." she said to a frazzled Grant.

He checked his phone. The time read *3:55.* So he sprinted outside the classroom and headed straight for the school door. As he burst through the doors of the school the first thing he saw was his mother's silver Nissan Altima. Inside he could see his mother's disapproving face. As Grant walked to the car, he kept his head low so no one would notice him. When he got in the car and sat down there was an awkward silence in the car.

"Hey mom..." he said softly to his mother

She remained silent as she pulled off from the school. During, the right Grant kept quiet and tried to prepare himself. However, he had no clue what to expect. He thought long and hard but all he knew to do was tell the truth.

The Truth

As Grant's mother pulled up to the police station. Grant's gut sunk not because of what was ahead of him but because in the parking spaces next to him was the car of George's mother and Brian's father.

Grant got out of the car and shut the door. As his mother walked in front Grant remained far behind. Inside the police, there were many on and off duty police officers, some of them working some of them laughing with each other.

"Hello may I help you" the lady at the front desk said to Grant's mother.

"We are here for questioning with Officer Diggs"

The woman at the desk quickly pointed to what seemed to be his office. Grant and his mother walked over to his door. Grant's mom quietly knocked on the door. Seconds later Officer Diggs popped out of the room and what do you know George comes rolling right out behind him. George's left arm and leg was sealed with a black cast and his neck was supported with a neck brace.

"Ms. Jane wonderful to see you again" Officer Diggs said

As Grant's mother conversed with Officer Diggs, Grant tried to get a word in with George.

"How are you doing?" Grant said to George as his body filled with guilt

George remained silent and just stared at Grant. After over 10 seconds of intense staring George uttered the words "This is your fault" and rolled off to his mother waiting by the doors of the police station. Grant tried to wave at George's mother however he was still in shock of what George just said to him. She shot him a mean-mugged look and walk out the door.

Grant sighed as guilt filled up his body.

"We're ready for you bud" Officer Diggs said to Grant as he welcomed him into his office

"Take a seat anywhere you'd like."

Grant sat in one of the two chairs he had directly in front of his desk. His mother sat in a chair behind him.

"So Grant have you ever done anything before like this?" Officer Diggs asked

"No sir" Grant replied

"Well it's simple all you have to do is answer my questions to the best of your ability and just... tell... the... truth." Officer digs explained

"OK first why where are you and Brian over George's house on the night of Halloween?"

"We were planning on going trick-or-treating together like we do every year."

"Did Brian enjoy trick-or-treating with you all or did he just do it because you all wanted him to?"

"No it was my understanding that Brian enjoy doing it with us just like he has every year."

"How did you all end up in the forest which was many blocks away from where you were originally trick-or-treating?"

"There was this old lady who we were trying to get away from she was acting very suspicious and we have wanted nothing to do with her so... We ran."

"No one saw where you were running and decided maybe that wasn't a good route to take?"

"I was running behind Brian and Brian was running behind George. So, I was not aware of where we were going I was just trying to get away."

"You're doing a great job so far" officer digs said "Did Brian act any different when he got into the forest "

"Yes, he was acting a little strange but we were all under the impression that that was just classic Brian being afraid of Dead Man's..."

"I beg your pardon", Officer Diggs said trying to hear what Grant said

Grant sighed because he knew it was already too late.

"Dead man's forest... That's what Brian called it at least. . that's why he was acting strange in the forest. Before we left to go trick-or-treating Brian explained to us how some old tale still went on to this day. How a man lived in the forest and would come after anybody who set foot on the grounds.

"Well, that is some useful information" Officer Diggs said "I think we have heard all we need for today"

Officer Diggs got up from his desk and walked to let Grant and his mother out the door.

"We will be in touch Ms. Jane" Officer Diggs said before shutting his door.

Search

Grant and his mother entered the car and drove home. Grant remained silent for the whole car ride reflecting on the information he gave to Officer Diggs. When Grant arrived home he exited the car and headed straight to his room. Most of the time, he only does this when he has stacks of homework to complete, but this time, he is still busy reflecting on the questioning wondering if he gave too much information to where the police would have suspicions about him.

Also, what did George say to the police? Would he lie on Grant? Would he tell them false information to cover himself? These all questions lingering in Grant's head. That were yet to be answered. Grant tried to clear his mind by going to take a shower and get ready for bed. However, he was still even thinking about it then.

After Grant got ready for bed he cleared his mind so he could get through the night.

Grant awoke to the subtle silence just like he had the morning before. Even the birds that normally sing a joyful tune were quiet. Grant got out of the bed and got ready for school just like any other day... or at least hoping for something close to it.

Grant headed down stairs with his book bag in hand not looking forward to another day.

"Good morning mom" Grant said as he entered the kitchen.

She remained quiet as Grant hesitantly ate some of the bacon off the plate that she prepared. Grant was pleasantly surprised and thought that maybe she had forgiven him for all that happened.

All of a sudden, she turned on the T.V. this was a surprise to Grant because normally she never did this so early in the morning. Grant's mother grabbed the remote and turned the volume up as the channel 5 news appeared on the screen.

Grant knew it could nothing be nothing could about to happen because his mother only watched the news when she knew something was going to be headlining.

"Listen" she said to Grant turning the volume up even more.

The news anchor began as a picture of the woods showed up in the top left screen. The bottom screen text read "BODY FOUND IN WOODS".

Grant did not know what to think of what he saw. Before saying anything he waited to hear what the anchor said.

"Breaking news today on this early morning. The police search for 13-year-old Brian O'Connell has come to an end. The young boy's body was found in the North Forest which some call Dead Man's Forest. Are prayers go out to the Friends and Family of this young man."

Grant took a seat to try and take the news. He could not help to cry. His best friend from elementary school is gone. Grant's mother walked over to Grant to comfort him. She rubbed his shoulder hugging him.

"I forgive you" she whispered in Grant's ear

The tears of Grant dripped down his face and onto the floor.

"You don't have to go to school today if you don't want to I know how middle schoolers can speculate" she said to Grant comforting him.

"NO... I need to go I need to face this because if I don't I will not be able to face anything else.

Grant got his book bag and headed out the door. He was ready to face this but at the same time he was scared. Grant walked to the bus stop and waited like every other day anyone who saw him would realize the crying he just did.

The bus pulled up and Grant got on. It was a weird silence on the bus. Normally when he got on the bus his ears filled with the screaming of children, but this time it was just...quiet. Grant walked down the isle of the bus and sat down in the first seat he saw. The bus ride went quickly as Grant was busy thinking of the fresh and bitter news.

Grant got off the bus and walked slowly into the school he entered and it was even more overwhelming than the day before. He walked to his locker avoiding everyone in the hallway. As he walked he felt the eyes of the kids on him. Grant could feel them watching him wondering why he was there in the first place. Grant reached his locker and entered his combination...

Click

Grant opened his locker and a pool of papers fell out. Grant's mouth was left hanging as he reached to see what the flyer was. The flyer read "DEAD MAN" with a picture of Brian. Grant dropped the flyer and ran to his first period class with tears falling down his face.

When he entered the class he went to the back of the class and put his head down on the desk. The pressure was getting to him he didn't feel that he could do it. His body was filled with guilt and he couldn't take. Grant knew what he had to do. He was debating it in his mind for a while and he knew that it was only right.

99

Suddenly, Grant made a dash for the doors leaving a trail of tears behind him.

Author's Note

The main character *Grant* was named after Carrington.

Fun Fact

Carrington is a native of Atlanta and has lived there his entire life.

Truancy

Grant burst out of the school doors with tears flowing down his face, guilt flowing down into the depths of his heart, and with shame lodged in his brain.

He didn't exactly know where he would go now that he was out of his living nightmare. All he knew was that he wasn't going back. He knew that this would happen eventually, nothing can go unknown at his school.

Grant walked off the school campus and went to find a seat somewhere to think things through. He sat at that bench for over thirty minutes contemplating his next move. Then it clicked in his mind. He knew what he had to do. Grant began to walk. He walked not knowing if he was even going the right direction. He was just walking. It was like he was being drawn to this place. As Grant reached his destination, he took a deep breath and looked at the sign above the entrance. He knew he was here. Grant gathered all his courage and entered the place where it all began. As he walked on the dead, crinkling leaves he reflected over everything that led him to this moment. Grant took a deep breath and said those words. Those three words that changed his life forever. He not only said them he screamed them at the top of his lungs...

Dead Man's Forest !!!"

Made in the USA
Las Vegas, NV
31 July 2021